It's Big Sister Time!

Written by **Nandini Ahuja**
Illustrated by **Catalina Echeverri**

HARPER FESTIVAL
An Imprint of HarperCollinsPublishers

To my parents, who taught me how to write, read, love, and be a sister.

To my sisters, who love to play dress up, get me out of trouble,
and want me on their team.

To my husband, who tells the funniest jokes, builds the coziest pillow forts,
and always lets me hold the popcorn.
—N. A.

To Felix and his Big Sister, Emilia
—C. E.

HarperFestival is an imprint of HarperCollins Publishers.

It's Big Sister Time!

Library of Congress Control Number: 2019944060
ISBN 978-0-06-288438-1

Typography by Honee Jang
20 21 22 23 24   RTLO   10 9 8 7 6 5 4 3 2 1
❖
First Edition

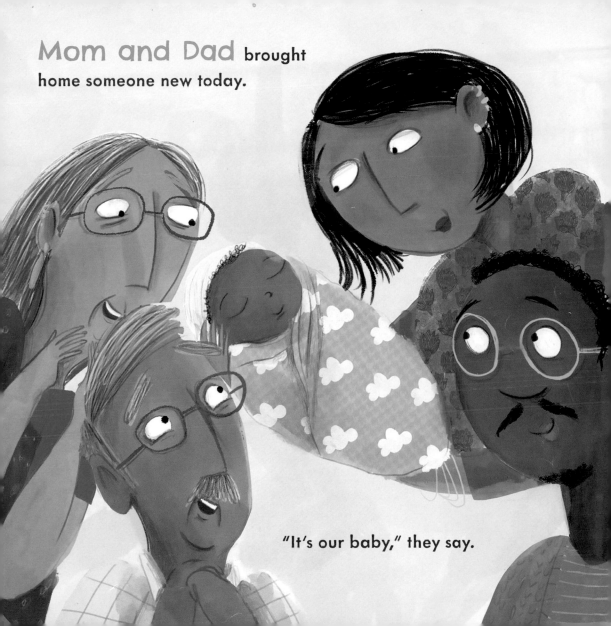

Mom and Dad brought
home someone new today.

"It's our baby," they say.

I ask Mom how long the baby
will be staying with us.
She says, "Forever!"

"Baby will be your new best friend."
I've never had a friend like *this.*

Baby's loud.

Baby's messy.

Sometimes Baby *really* smells.

Maybe Baby doesn't know
the house rules yet.

I tell Dad that he should probably have a talk with Baby.

But Dad says, "You'll have to teach Baby the rules since you're the big sister."

I guess I can help Baby
learn the rules.

After all, I was a baby too.
And I was *really* good at it.

Rule number one: There's absolutely no playing with my toys.

Even if you choose one first

. . . unless I say so.

At nap time, you can't sleep with my *big* girl blankie.

Even if it's just the right size for you.

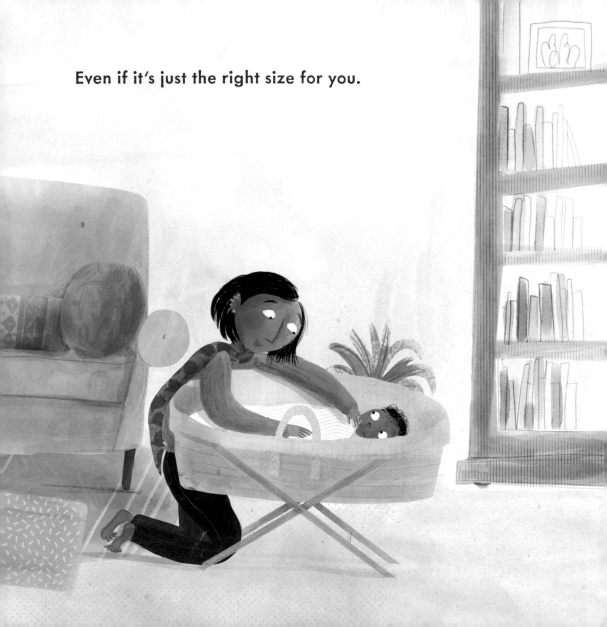

When Grandma and Grandpa
come over to make rice pudding,
I get to be their helper.

Even if you get the chef's hat.

You've got to put Mom's scarves away
before she gets home from work.

Even if you're in the middle of fighting crime.

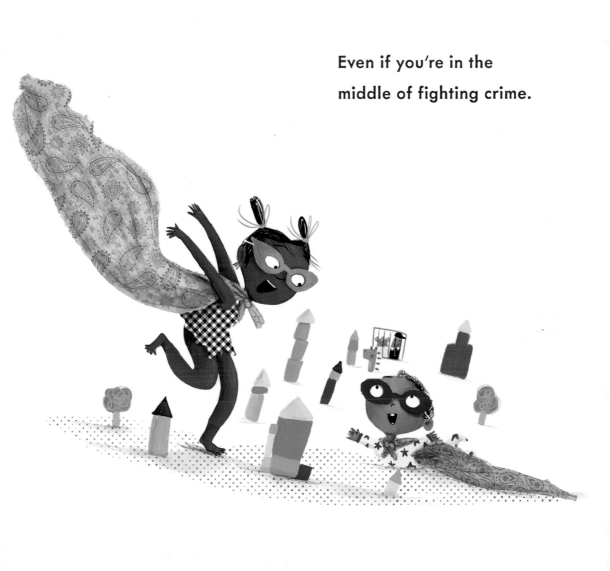

There's no building pillow forts at bedtime, especially after getting tucked in.

Even though pillow forts
are really cozy.

On movie night, I get to sit between
Mom and Dad and hold the popcorn.

But I guess I can hold you instead.

When my friends come over to play,
you have to be on my team.

Even if they ask nicely.

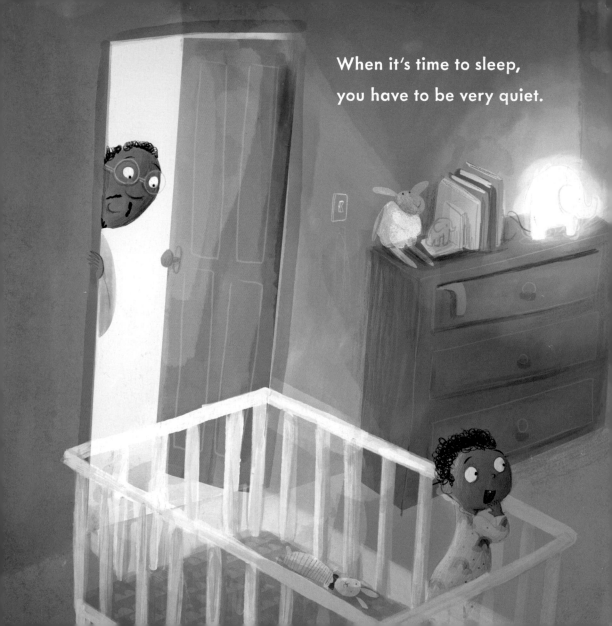

When it's time to sleep,
you have to be very quiet.

Even if someone tells a really funny joke.

If you accidentally make a mess,
you can ask me for help.

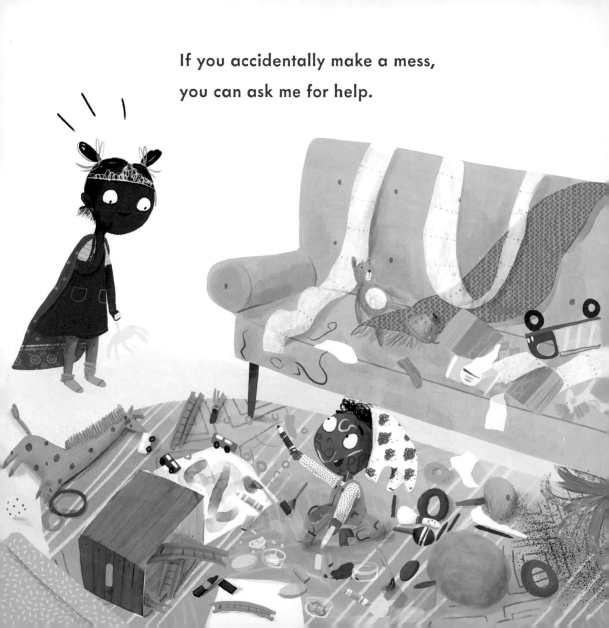

Even if it's a *big* mess.

The last and most important rule is,
no matter what, we stick together.

Because . . .

we're a team now.